THOMAS & FRIENDS™

Thomas and the Shark

Based on the Railway Series
by the Reverend W Awdry

Illustrated by Richard Courtney

Random House New York

Thomas is
at Brendam Docks.
All the engines
are very busy today.

There is a lot of cargo.
They must take it
around Sodor.

Percy picks up mail.

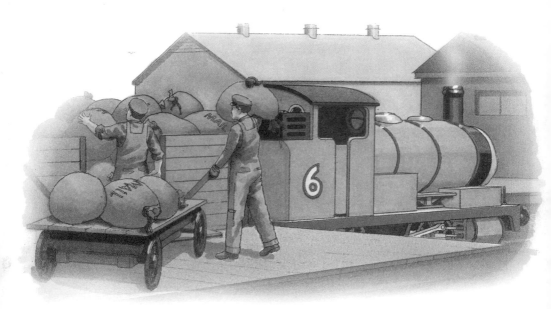

Henry picks up steel.

Thomas picks up flour.
It is almost time
to get moving.

But then
all the engines
crowd around Salty.

Thomas cannot see
what is going on.
He asks James.
"Salty has a shark!"
says James.

Salty will take the shark
to the Sodor aquarium.
It will live there
with other sea animals.

Thomas wants
to see the shark.
The other engines
are in his way!

Thomas cannot wait
any longer.
He has work to do.
He leaves the docks.

The other engines stay
to see the shark.
They try
to get closer.

Gordon wants
to get the closest.
He bumps
Cranky's hook.

Cranky's hook bumps
into the shark car.
The shark car
comes loose!

The shark car
rolls away.
It starts to roll
down a hill.

Oh, no!

Salty must stop it.

The shark car rolls
and rolls.
It moves faster
and faster.
Salty chases it.

The shark car goes
over a bridge.

It goes
into a tunnel.
Gordon tries
to catch it.

Percy tries, too.
The shark car goes
around a bend.
It is moving fast!

James and Emily
try to help.

None of the engines
can catch up.
The shark car
is too fast!

Thomas is on his way
to the bakery.
He is still sad that
he missed the shark.

He hears peeps
and shouts.

Thomas stops.
He looks
up the hill.

He sees the shark!
It is rolling right
toward him.

Thomas speeds up.
He gets in front
of the shark car.
He drops flour
on the track.

The flour slows down
the shark car.
Thomas stops the shark!

Salty and the other
engines catch up.
Salty thanks Thomas.
All the engines cheer.

"Will you take
the shark
to the aquarium?"
Salty asks Thomas.

Thomas says yes.
He delivers the shark
safe and sound.
Thomas is a hero!

Dear Parents:

Congratulations! Your child is taking the first steps on an exciting journey. The destination? Independent reading!

STEP INTO READING® will help your child get there. The program offers five steps to reading success. Each step includes fun stories and colorful art or photographs. In addition to original fiction and books with favorite characters, there are Step into Reading Non-Fiction Readers, Phonics Readers and Boxed Sets, Sticker Readers, and Comic Readers—a complete literacy program with something to interest every child.

Learning to Read, Step by Step!

Ready to Read   Preschool–Kindergarten
• big type and easy words • rhyme and rhythm • picture clues
For children who know the alphabet and are eager to begin reading.

Reading with Help   Preschool–Grade 1
• basic vocabulary • short sentences • simple stories
For children who recognize familiar words and sound out new words with help.

Reading on Your Own   Grades 1–3
• engaging characters • easy-to-follow plots • popular topics
For children who are ready to read on their own.

Reading Paragraphs   Grades 2–3
• challenging vocabulary • short paragraphs • exciting stories
For newly independent readers who read simple sentences with confidence.

Ready for Chapters   Grades 2–4
• chapters • longer paragraphs • full-color art
For children who want to take the plunge into chapter books but still like colorful pictures.

STEP INTO READING® is designed to give every child a successful reading experience. The grade levels are only guides; children will progress through the steps at their own speed, developing confidence in their reading.

Remember, a lifetime love of reading starts with a single step!

Thomas the Tank Engine & Friends™

CREATED BY BRITT ALLCROFT

Based on the Railway Series by the Reverend W Awdry.
© 2013 Gullane (Thomas) LLC.
Thomas the Tank Engine & Friends and Thomas & Friends are trademarks of
Gullane (Thomas) LLC. Thomas the Tank Engine & Friends and Design Is Reg. U.S. Pat. &
Tm. Off. © 2013 HIT Entertainment Limited.

Step into Reading, Random House, and the Random House colophon are registered trademarks
of Penguin Random House LLC.

Visit us on the Web!
StepIntoReading.com
rhcbooks.com
www.thomasandfriends.com

Educators and librarians, for a variety of teaching tools, visit us at
RHTeachersLibrarians.com

ISBN: 978-0-307-98200-1

Printed in the United States of America
16 15 14 13 12 11 10 9 8 7

HIT entertainment